FOR THEA
X X

First published 2020 by Two Hoots
an imprint of Pan Macmillan
The Smithson, 6 Briset Street, London EC1M 5NR
Associated companies throughout the world
www.panmacmillan.com
ISBN 978-1-5098-8984-6
Text and illustrations copyright © Morag Hood 2020
Moral rights asserted.

1 3 5 7 9 8 6 4 2
A CIP catalogue record for this book is available from the British Library.
Printed in China
The illustrations in this book were painted in gouache and then digitally coloured.

www.twohootsbooks.com

MORAG HOOD
SPAGHETTI HUNTERS

TW🦉 HOOTS

Duck was looking for his spaghetti.

It was not going well.

"NEVER FEAR!"

said Tiny Horse.

"For I am the greatest
spaghetti hunter there
has ever been and
I shall save the day."

"Spaghetti is the trickiest of all the pastas," said Tiny Horse.

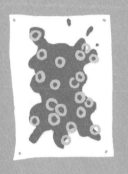

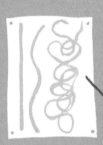

"It can be almost impossible to find."

"But I have all the things we need."

WANTED

"SPAGHETTI"
-LONG
-THIN
-YELLOW
-TASTY

REWARD

PEANUT BUTTER

"The spaghetti will
not escape us."

And so the Great Spaghetti Hunt began.

It was a bit
different to how
Duck had imagined.

"I know what I'm
doing," said Tiny Horse.

But Duck couldn't find any spaghetti.
Until . . .

"I have triumphed," said Tiny Horse,

"I present . . ."

"SPAGHETTI!"

Duck did not remember spaghetti
being quite so green or stringy,
and he especially did not like the
way it was hissing at him.

"NONE OF THESE ARE SPAGHETTI!"

said Duck.

"Not even close. This one is an **EARWIG**."

"I'm going back to my teapot."

And Duck stomped off to find a book to read.

"Books are not as good as
spaghetti," said Tiny Horse,

who had come along even though
no-one had invited her.

But this book was a bit different.

Tiny Horse was not impressed.

"This is not standard spaghetti
hunting equipment," she said.

"You can't just
MAKE spaghetti."

PASTA
3 EGGS
FLOUR

1. MIX EGGS + FLOUR
2. KNEAD
3. REST
4. MAKE PASTA

"It does look, taste and feel a bit like spaghetti," said Tiny Horse.

"Although perhaps
it is a little dry ..."

"BUT NEVER FEAR!"

said Tiny Horse.

"FOR I SHALL HUNT DOWN THAT MOST FEARSOME OF BEASTS..."

"TOMATO SAUCE."